PUMPKINHEADS

PUMPKINHEADS

WRITTEN BY

RAINBOW ROWELL

ILLUSTRATED BY

FAITH ERIN HICKS

COLOR BY SARAH STERN

:01

First Second
NEW YORK

1

LAST NIGHT AT THE PATCH

4

5

Deja. The Succotash Hut is this way.

I know. I've worked there for three years.

So, where are *you* going?

The Pie Palace.

What?

SUCCOT
PIE PA

Josie, when you look back at your time at the Patch, what's the *one* thing you're going to regret?

Letting Meredith Gomez win MVPPP last September.

You couldn't help that— you had walking pneumonia!

I could still *walk*.

Okay, what's the *other* thing you're going to regret?

Oh. *The Fudge Girl.*

In three years, I feel like you could have come up with a better nickname...

She works in the Fudge Shoppe.

I'm well aware.

Tonight is your *last* chance to talk to her.

I *can't* talk to her, Deja. You know I can't.

Josie, you *have* to. You've been mooning over her—loudly and at length—for three years. You can't just *never* talk to her.

I can. I *will*.

That's the plan, actually.

That's *not* the plan.

Fortunately, bunny boy, your best friend is looking out for you—I'm not going to let you miss the last hayrack ride of the night.

Is that a metaphor?

It is. Tonight, on your dinner break, you are going to *talk* to that girl.

And she? Is going to see how cute and nice you are. You're going to *take your shot.*

I don't know—

Don't let me down, Josie. I had to give Jaden and Aidan twenty dollars and three free hot-dog coupons to trade shifts.

Did you tell them why?

I told them I like pie. Which is true.

11

2

PANIC AT THE PIE PALACE

It was never a campaign. It was a lifestyle.

I love it when you alliterate.

Well, we're not here for any Pie Palace pantry improvement projects.

Presently.

We're *here* to salvage your romantic future.

T minus five minutes, by the way.

FUDGE SHOPPE

I already told you: I'm your *friend.* And friends don't let friends live small lives.

Why are you putting me up to this? You never cared about my "romantic future" before.

"Hi, I'm Josiah, I've memorized your schedule."

Deja. Seriously. I need your help.

Okay, okay. Let's role-play this. Pretend I'm Superfudge, and just... start a conversation.

Okay, um...

"Hi, I'm Josiah."

"Hi, I'm the Fudge Shoppy Girl, known to my friends as Marcy."

Marcy...

Maybe don't repeat her name dreamily like she's just handed you the One Ring.

Right. Right. Okay...

"It's nice to meet you. Marcy."

"I think I've seen you around. Don't you sell okra casserole on the wrong side of the miniature train tracks?"

"Y-yes."

And...

"ITALKALOTABOUT YOURFACE!"

18

Let's try again: This time I'll be you, and you be Elmer Fudge.

But I don't know her— I don't know what she'd say.

Just roll with it...

"Hii, I'm Josiuhhh."

Suddenly I have a Southern accent?

"Hi. I'm Josiah."

"Hi. I'm Marcy. I guess."

"I work on the other side of the park, and I've always meant to talk to you."

Oh, that's good! I should write that down.

"I know tonight is our last night, and you're working. But maybe you'd like to hang out sometime?"

"I'm a really nice guy, and I swear I'll stop acting like such a dork after you get to know me."

Should I say all of that?

Maybe don't say that last part.

Argggh! It doesn't matter what I say! Why would she say yes? Why would she even want to know me?

Deja? Did I lose you?

Look at all this pie I've never tried, and tonight is my very last night to do it. I should have planned this better...

FUDGE SHOPPE

3

NEXT STOPPE: FUDGE SHOPPE

I don't have to do this just because you're telling me to.

Everything about our friendship so far says otherwise.

I'm my own man!

You've forced my hand, Josie. As the Succotash Hut shift manager, I am ordering you—

You're pulling rank on me? We take *turns* being manager so that we can both put it on our résumés!

Well, tonight's my night. Go get her, champ. Seize the day.

PIE PALACE

Bring me back some fudge!

That isn't a metaphor!

Thanks, hon, what can I do you for?

Is...um... is Marcy here?

She's filling in down at the S'mores Pit tonight. The whole Patch is swamped. Can I help you?

Uh, no... Thanks.

GIRLS J
WANNA H
FUDGE

Oh, no...

She rejected you?

She wasn't there to reject me. She's working down at the S'mores Pit tonight.

The S'mores Pit! How does this girl get all the best gigs...

WHUMP

Anyway. Thanks for trying.

Josie. Are you really giving up because of a *change of venue*?

SHOOM

Well, what am I supposed to do? Run down there as soon as the Patch closes?

4

EX MARKS
THE SPOT

Do we have time?

This is my last chance to have a double-dipped Granny Smith. We'll make time.

You can always come back to the Patch some weekend as a guest, remember?

Maybe we should stop by the Succotash Hut while we're out, just to check on things.

We really *don't* have time for that—

Hide me.
There's my ex.

Which
one?

Jess.
Don't look.

Which
Jess?

The sigher.

Deja!

Jess! Hey!

Hey, Jess.

Hi, Josiah.

How's life at the the Pony-Go-Round?

Oh, you know...

SIGH

They put that chili fry stand across from us, and now people try to feed the ponies chili fries. It's really unfortunate: Ponies are vegetarians.

SIGH

There's a new chili fry stand?

I stopped by the Succotash Hut earlier to say good-bye, but you weren't there. It was a real scene.

What kind of scene...

The Patch won't be the same without you next year, Deja.

SIGH

SIGH

All the best people are seniors.

Josie and I are going to come back next year as guests. We'll have to stop by for a pony ride.

Nobody over seven is allowed to ride the ponies.

I was just kidding, Jess.

Oh.

SIGH

Right.

You were always so funny.

Right. So... I'm going to buy this caramel apple.

PAPPY'S APPLES

A CARAMEL APPLE A DAY HELPS YOUR DENTIST

Okay... Good-bye, Deja. Have a beautiful life.

Thanks, Jess. Right back atcha!

5
STOP, THIEF!

How did you date Jess? She's so...not smart.

She's plenty smart. She's just...more of a pony person than a people person.

DING DING DING

What did she mean, that the Succotash Hut is "a real scene"?

Probably just that it's busy. The whole park is a mob scene tonight.

DING DING

I can't believe that kid stole my caramel apple!

I can't believe you tried to follow him onto the tracks!

I'm going to END that little twerp.

PAT PAT

Yeah you are.

But *first* I'm going to get another caramel apple.

So we both agree that Mission: Fudge Girl is a dead end?

6

S'MORE PROBLEMS

I always get turned around down here. Which way is the S'mores Pit?

GREAT PUMPKIN SLINGSHOT
HAUNTED HACIENDA
GRANDMA'S CHICKEN RA—

INHALE

That way.

How do you know?

Where there's smoke, there's s'mores.

You're acting like I'm marching you to your death, not the girl of your dreams. Don't you *want* to meet Vanilla Fudge?

Sort of. I mean, I already like her so much— what's the point of meeting her?

What if our relationship has already peaked?

You don't have a relationship.

You're right. And my favorite part of our non-relationship is the fact that she's never rejected me.

You better make yourself a s'more right away. When she starts laughing at me, I'm going to want to make a quick retreat.

Good thinking, Josie.

P.S. Girls actually *like* it when cute guys ask them out.

Yeah, but I'm not a "cute guy."

I call 'em like I see 'em.

Hey, Dave, how's it going?

It's a nightmare! Did you hear we're oversold? I don't know how they expect us to work like this!

It's not a sword, it's a marshmallow skewer!

KLAK

KLAK

Hey, is, um, Marcy down here tonight?

Why? Are you finally going to tell her about your little crush?

I wouldn't call it a *little* crush, Dave.

Well, you're out of luck. She went to get more marshmallows, and they ended up keeping her at the Kettle Corn Kettle. I guess it's a riot up there, too.

Did you hear what happened at the Petting Zoo? Somebody let out *Buck!*

They let out *Buck?*

There will be blood.

Those are red-hot pokers, you demons!

KLAK

KLAK

Here, take over for a minute.

It's like you hate having eyes!

You seem to be in a bit of a situation.

TOSS

If you don't put your sticks down, I'll eat all these marshmallows myself!

Looks like you already did!

PLOP

Hey, kid, there's your marshmallow.

7

DEJA VU

Hey. Deja. Do you know where we are?

The S'mores Pit?

This is where we first met! At new employee orientation.

That's right...

I thought it was cool!

You didn't.

Well... I thought it was *funny*.

And you felt so sorry for me that you consented to be my partner.

I didn't feel sorry for you, Josie—I'm not that nice.

Two succotash legends were born that night.

Argh. That's also the first time I saw Fudge Girl. Though she was just "Pretty Pink Headband Girl" then...

Aarrrgh.

Graham-cracker me.

What is it about that girl?

What do you mean?

What keeps so you so... I don't know, *enthralled* after all this time? You've never even talked to her.

I'm not sure. I saw her that night and something *clicked*—

I liked the way she looked. The way she walked. The way she seemed...

Seemed what?

Just the way she *seemed*. Like, it's really easy to imagine good things about her.

I can't decide if that's hopelessly romantic. Or just hopeless.

I always have a better night if I catch a glimpse of her, you know? It makes me feel lucky somehow.

Josiah.

Yeah?

What would happen if we *didn't* go back to the Pie Palace?

Uh...we'd get in trouble?

Probably not.

Why *wouldn't* we go back?

Because we're on a *mission*.

I've decided that you're going to talk to Vanessa Fudgens tonight. And once I've set my mind on something, I won't be dissuaded.

You're suggesting that we just skip...*work*?

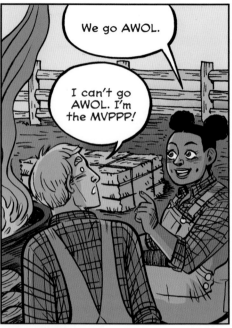

We go AWOL.

I can't go AWOL. I'm the MVPPP!

It's just a few hours. And those pie people hardly know us. They'll probably think we're filling in somewhere else.

But they need our help.

Filling in, get it? Pies? Filling?

It seems really irresponsible...

It seems *bold*.

No. I can't skip work.

Hey, can you guys help me through the after-dinner rush?

Sorry you missed Marcy, Josiah. Maybe you can talk to a girl in your next life.

I'm a girl, Dave.

All right. We go AWOL, and we *find* her.

Well, we already know where she is... but YES!

8
PSL
(PUMPKIN SPICE LIFE)

What?

The smell.

All I'm getting right now is ponies. It's like I'm still dating Jess.

SNFF SNFF

The ponies are part of it. But, also, there's smoke...

There is a *lot* of smoke tonight. What's up with that?

And cotton candy. The cider mulling, the turkey legs roasting—

We still haven't had dinner...

Even the straw and the leaves rotting... The Patch smells like *fall*, you know?

Like every autumn smell all at once.

Next year, at college, fall is going to smell so flat.

Aw, Josie, I'll send you a scented candle.

It won't be the same.

THMP THMP THMP THMP THMP THMP

KATHUNK SNORT KATHUNK KATHNK KATHNK

9

COOL, COOL, COOL

All right, Josie-boy, here's the plan: We're going to march right up to that Kettle Corn Kettle...

...and we are going to *get* ourselves some kettle corn.

Not the bagged kind, either— fresh out of the kettle.

That's the plan?

My mission tonight is to eat as many of my favorite Patch snacks as possible.

I thought your mission was to help me meet Fudge Girl?

It is! But the snacks are a new side mission. We've got the whole night ahead of us now!

I don't see her...

She can't have moved on already. That'd be ridiculous.

THMP THMP THMP

81

My friend's trying to seize the day.

I'm not Marcy.

No, I know, but is she here?

Carpe diem, etc.

Is that her?

Uh...no.

Then no.

Before we leave you to your work, could I just get a small, complimentary sample?

Now beat it.

SCOOP

Hey. Josie.

GOTTA KRAVIN FOR MORE KETTLE CORN? CHECK OUT OUR NEW LOCATION BY THE PUMPKIN DROP!

We came to the wrong Kettle.

Yep. Let's go.

Deja, that's on the other side of the park...

We've got nothing but time! It's seven o'clock— the Patch doesn't close for three hours!

We'll cut through Gourdy Golf, go around the Freeto pie stand, then take the employee shortcut through the corn maze...

...and we'll still have time for a Pumpkin Bomb after you get Cornelius Fudge's number!

What's a Pumpkin Bomb?

JOSIAH! You've never had a Pumpkin Bomb?!

Vanilla ice cream sandwiched between two wedges of pumpkin pie, on a stick, dipped in chocolate...

We have so much to accomplish tonight. Thank goodness we decided not to work!

GOURDY GOLF

HOLE #6 PAR 4

PAR FOR THE GOURD

SQUASHED

Deja!

Jess!

Ah. Cool Jess.

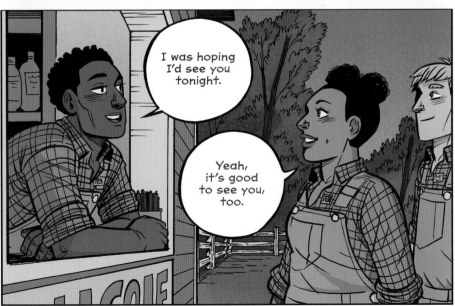

I was hoping I'd see you tonight.

Yeah, it's good to see you, too.

Cool...

Cool...

Hey, Josie and I just need to cut across the golf course, for... work purposes, so...

You know, some of us are going out after we close tonight—

To an after-hours pumpkin patch?

Ha! Nah. Just, you know, Jenny's house. Her parents are cool with it.

Cool.

Yeah, you should come.

Thanks. I mean, maybe. Josie and I usually go to Walgreens on Halloween after work.

They're marking down the candy *right now*.

Right, cool, well if you change your mind...

Cool!

Cool!

Cool!

GOURDY GO

I can't remember— why'd you break up with *that* Jess? He's always so chill.

He was *too* chill, it made me nervous. Plus he listens to his own podcast in the car.

How have you dated half the pumpkin patch, and I haven't made any progress at all with Fudge Shoppe Girl?

Poc!

Because I actually talk to people?

Kick!

HOLE IN ONE!

It's easy for you—you're beautiful, and everybody likes you.

It's not *that* easy.

It is. I've seen you in action—

"Hi, I'm Deja. I need somebody to follow me around and listen to me be great. You look like a good candidate."

And that's it. They're hooked.

You think I'm great?

Everybody thinks you're great. *And* you have dimples. I'd be a different man if I had dimples.

Well, Josie, if you really think I'm great, think about *this*: In the three seasons I've worked at this pumpkin patch, I've always asked to work with you.

You were *assigned* to work with me.

The first time. After that, it was a choice.

Wait, we can ask for different assignments every season?

Of course we can. Seniority counts.

Then why are we stuck at the Succotash Hut?

Because *you* choose it every year!

I didn't know we could move! *Deja.* We could have been working in the Haunted Hacienda.

Why would you want to work there? People puke in the Poltergeist Tunnel!

Besides, I thought you *loved* the Succotash Hut.

I do, I do. But I feel like I could have made a bigger impact in a higher profile attraction. The pedal cars!

Only football players work the pedal cars. You have to be able to lift the cars if they tip over on someone.

Well, we could have been *someplace* other than the Succotash Hut. We could have been in the *Fudge Shoppe*.

10

SUCCOTASH-TROPHE

What have they done to our succotash?!

How could they mess this up? Actual monkeys could make succotash.

That's not true; there's a technique.

The technique is *stirring*.

We've got to fix this.

No! Josie! If we stop to help them, there's no way they'll let us go. We're on a mission!

They're going to burn down our hut!

The hut will come back bigger and better!

They're sullying the reputation of our succotash!

After tonight, it won't be "our succotash" anymore.

We're not staying. We just came to give you some succotash advice.

Why aren't you stirring, Jaden? You should be stirring!

Like heck you're not staying!

You squirt in some water, and then you stir. It's a dance: Squirt, stir. Squirt, stir.

You squirt and stir. We're getting out of this dump.

You spend your whole life in a Pie Palace, never knowing an honest day's work...

Hey...why aren't *you guys* at the Pie Palace?

Oh, snap.

What do you want to do, Josie?

Stay and make these people some delicious succotash.

Okay, boys, fine. Go back to your Palace. We'll just—

—make a break for it!

What about the succotash?

For God's sake, Josie— true love trumps lima beans!

11

MAKE LIKE
A TREE
AND LEAF

12

TOUR DE PUMPKIN

≋Huff≋

I'm not questioning your decision to run.

But we could have run *in the direction* of the Kettle Corn Kettle.

We've just taken a slight detour.

Which way now?

Around the world.

We'll take a shortcut, just past the Pumpkin Tower!

TOUR DE PUMPK

I heard he dragged a fifth-grader through the corn maze.

I heard he ate her ponytail.

I heard Mr. DeKnock put a fifty-dollar bounty on his head—fifty dollars and five free hot-dog coupons.

Wanted. Dead or alive.

I'm pretty sure they want Buck alive—he's just a goat.

Hey, Deja.

Brian, my friend! Can Josie and I cut the line? It's our last night.

Be my guest...

Pedal harder, Josie!

But we're going to miss the shortcut!

Just...a... few more... feet.

Deja, this isn't part of the mission!

This is *vengeance!* Vengeance is an unspoken part of every mission!

But my Fudge Shoppe Girl!

This isn't over!

SHOOM

TURN

I hope Jaden and Aidan don't turn us in. Do you think anybody's looking for us? I'm probably going to lose MVPPP over this.

Honestly, I don't think anyone will care.

I *deserve* to lose MVPPP. I'm putting my own needs before the needs of the Patch!

Meredith Gomez is probably delivering a baby in the corn maze right now.

Or teaching thirty Girl Scouts how to make pumpkin butter.

Think of tonight as part of your transition, Josie. You have to move on. You can't stay at the Patch forever.

Todd did. He's been working at the Patch since it opened. Every season! And he's a certified public accountant now.

You don't want to be like Todd! He won't even take his mascot costume off at parties.

The man loves his job.

The man loves wearing a giant pumpkin head. It's like talking to a mime.

Trust me, you don't want to be MVPPP sixteen years in a row.

Think of how many stars there'd be on my nametag...

The world is full of stars, Josie. And also nametags.

Pardon me, are you in line?

No.

Yes.

FREE TO PIE

FREE TO PIE STOP

Relax— we still have *hours* to get to the Kettle Corn Kettle.

13

CHEESY COME,
CHEESY GO

Hey there, little kitten, what's wrong?

WAHHHHHH!!!

Do you know where your mom and dad are?

NOOOOOO!

I'll bet we can find them.

The goooastesses came, and I ran away. I'm scared of goooooastesses!!!

WAAAAHHHHHH!!!

Aw, you don't have to worry about ghosts. Ghosts aren't real.

But I saw it! It tried to eat the lady!

But—

Don't argue with her, she knows what she saw.

We're going to help you find your parents. Okay?

WAHHH

Come on, kiddo, it's going to be all right. Are you hungry?

I've got some candy corn.

I can't take candy from strangers!!!

Oh, right. That's smart.

But I can take... ≶sniff≶

...some Freeto pie.

Really? Are you sure the same rule doesn't apply?

Come on, we'll go back and get you another one. I'm hungry, too.

Why doesn't God want me to have snacks?

I'll let you take the bounty for this. Finding a lost kid is primo MV-triple-P fodder.

Willa!

MOMMY!

I was so worried about you!

I thought the goastesses ate you!

I'm so glad I could help you find your daughter, ma'am. All in a day's work.

You didn't find her, Meredith. *We* found her.

I found the *mom*.

The mom wasn't lost!

Are you hungry?

I gave her my dinner— I hope that was okay.

Of course. Thank you...

Deja.

Looks like *I'm* suddenly in the running for MVPPP. I'll thank you both in my acceptance speech.

You don't get to give a speech.

Heyyy, what are you guys doing so far from the Succotash Hut...

Dinner break.

Kind of late for a dinner break...

What are *you* doing so far from the Succotash Hut?

I don't work at the Succotash Hut.

Exactly.

Happy Halloween, Meredith!

14

MAIZED AND CONFUSED

THE TWISTIEST CORN MAZE HEARTLAND!

WELCOME

GET LOST!

Hey, Deja. Josiah.

Tim!

Tim.

You guys on break?

Yep! Thought we'd take a stroll through the maze.

I'm headed back to Mission Control.

Gotta dead walkie.

Better take care of that.

Thank you, I will. You going to Jenny's later?

No.

Maybe...

Then maybe I'll see you there.

Y'all be careful in there. You know the employee shortcut?

Left, left, right, right— it's the same every year.

If you get lost, just call me. You still got my number?

Got it.

Well, all right.

He was *this* close to calling you "little lady."

What did you ever see in him?

What's your deal with Tim? He seems like your cup of tea— he's devoted to the Patch. He's worked here since high school.

He's devoted to *himself.* The Patch is just part of his whole...*scheme.*

Scheme?

He's got a scheme! He wants to run this place like a Six Flags!

Tim is the reason we outsource our pumpkin bread.

136

He said it wasn't appropriate for someone in management to date an hourly employee...

Which will only be a conflict of interest for another seventy-five minutes...

You.

GRAB

We lost him.

Maybe if we listen...

He's long gone, Deja.

NOOOOO!

That little criminal has made a fool of me TWICE.

I'm going to get him banned for life.

How? We don't have a picture of him...

I'll *draw* a picture.

All I wanted to do tonight was help you talk to that dumb girl and get myself some snacks.

Here.

I can't take your dinner, Josie. I'm not some snot-faced thief...

I *will* share it with you, however.

Do you really think Fudge Shoppe Girl is dumb?

Oh, I don't know. I don't know anything about her.

She doesn't *seem* dumb.

From a distance?

You know what I mean...

I really don't.

I can't ever get a sense of someone until I meet them.

So...you've never had a crush on a stranger?

People all sort of look the same to me until I talk to them. That's when they start to get interesting. That's when they start to... *shimmer*.

Fudge Girl— M-Marcy— was shimmering when we met. That's *why* I noticed her.

So you crush on her all year long?

No. I guess not. It's more of a Patch thing. Like, it's one of the things I get excited about every fall...

Josie—do you think *we're* going to hang out after this?

You and me? Of course! I mean, if you want.

We never have before. We never even talk off-season.

CRUMPLE

I didn't think **you** wanted to. I figured you had plenty of winter-spring-summer friends...

I **do.**

Well, I thought I was just your Patch friend.

You **are.**

But we could be outside-of-the-Patch friends, too. We could be friends for all seasons.

If that's what you want, yeah. In the middle of summer.

You mean we could get together, and, like, *recreationally* make succotash?

Deja?

Yeah?

Do you know how to get out of here?

We can just backtrack, right?

Which way did we come from?

Ughhhhhhhh. I'm sorry I got so distracted. How much time do we have left?

It doesn't matter. If we don't make it to the Kettle Corn Kettle in time, then it wasn't meant to be.

There you go *again*, Josie.

It's not *fate* that brings people together. It's *people!*

You keep acting like you have no control over your love life!

Deja, I've never even had a love life.

This maze doesn't get to decide whether you and Fudge Judy are meant to be. Or whether you talk to her.

You do.

And you're not giving up.

NOD

I don't know what you have against fate. Fate brought us together. You and me.

But fate brought us to the Patch...

No, our individual needs and desires brought us to the Patch. *I* needed a job, and *you* love decorative gourds.

I brought us together. I sat down next to you.

C'mon, you love this place as much as I do...

Again, not fate. It's not coincidence that two people who love pumpkin patches ended up at one...

THIS WAY OUT

OR IS IT THIS WAY?

It was a series of choices: We *chose* to work together. I *chose* to keep working together...

We *choose* to be friends.

I didn't choose to be your friend.

Now you tell me.

No,
I mean—
I can't help it.

While that's
very sweet,
Josie, it isn't
actually true...

You choose to be my
friend every day that
you show up. And I
choose to be yours.

That makes it
sound like work!
I'd rather think
we were meant to
be friends.

But if I felt the same way that you do, we never would have met!

I would have waited for fate to deliver a friend to me instead of sitting down next to you.

Maybe—stick with me here—maybe *that's* why we were meant to be friends.

I was *meant* to meet someone who would take the initiative.

Oh, so you were destined to meet somebody who would do all the work?

Says the girl who lets me make the succotash.

I'm better with customers, okay? You're better with okra!

Shhh!

I'm better with customers. You're better with okra.

...ALL MY BAGS ARE PACKED, I'M READY TO GO...

Deja! John Colorado Springs plays their last show down by the Pumpkin Drop!

Which is right next to the Kettle Corn Kettle! We've got to be close!

But, Josie, we're still lost...

SHF

SHF

SHF

163

Josiah Templeton! You're cheating!

We weren't in here for the challenge!

But this damages the maze!

The maze gets steamrolled tomorrow!

We're going to get corn lice!

You're making that up!

15
LAST CHANCE, JOSIE

Sorry, Josiah. Marcy wanted to catch the last hayrack ride.

She said she'd never been on it, the whole time she's worked here! Isn't that sad?

Yeah.

Sad.

WHEW

Well...thanks, for trying to help me.

What? This isn't over. We know where she is. Go! Now! You can still make it!

Deja, it's pointless! She probably would have rejected me anyway!

You said it was!

Probably. But that's not the point! This isn't about true love forever.

It's about reaching for the things you want in life!

It's about being the flipper, not the pinball!

The flipper?

I don't want this girl to achieve *mythical status* in your life just because you never talked to her.

HAY RACK RIDE

hff hff

hff hff

LEAP

Oh, hey, Todd.

HRK!

FWUMP

Maybe we could talk later?

16

CARPE HAYRACK!

SHUNK

snort

SNORT!

WSSH

This is
really dangerous
and against
the rules.

SNORT!

SNORT!

SNORT

Josiah!

Hi, my name is Josiah.

You know my name.

Your picture's all over the break room.

It's fine.

I guess I'm just bummed because it's my last night at the Patch and—

Me, too. I'm going to miss working here so much!

Oh God, that's not what I meant—I *hate* this place.

You do?

Yes. It's always cold. And dirty—this is basically a dirt-rack ride.

And everything's so lame and tacky.

The signs. The scarecrows, these stupid overalls...

I guess you could call it tacky. Or...you *could* call it charming and authentic.

Authentically *gross*. I won't get the smell of fudge out of my hair until December.

Who doesn't like the smell of fudge...

You should hear the nicknames people come up with when you work in the Fudge Shoppe for three years.

I mean...

I don't understand—if you hate everything about the Patch, why are you sad that it's your last night?

And I don't even like pumpkins! Did you know in Germany they're pig food?

Because I'll miss my friends.

They're the only reason I work here. We're all going to different colleges next year...

We were supposed to ride the hayrack together tonight, on our dinner break—but then I got sent all over the place.

I didn't even get to spend my last night here with the people I really care about.

Josiah! Where are you going?

Back.

Back?

I'm on a mission.

That's extremely dangerous!

And against the rules, I know! I feel bad about it!

17

PUMPKIN
BOMB

Todd! Hey! Where do you get Pumpkin Bombs?

OM NOM
NOM

PAT PAT

Yeah, yeah. Where?

Deja!

hff

Josie... What happened? Did you miss her?

No. And I'm not going to.

I don't understand.

I caught up with her. I talked to her.

To the Fudge Girl?

To Marcy.

No. She's the object of your confection.

Get it? *Confection?* Because she works in the Fudge Shoppe.

She *was.* I know. But now I've talked to her, and... I'm not going to miss her. I'm going to miss the pumpkin patch. And I'm going to miss YOU.

I know, Josie—

No. You don't. I'm going to *miss* you, Deja. Like... *really.*

You're my best friend! You're better than my winter-spring-summer friends.

You're better than anyone I know.

Deja.
I don't want October to be over. Because October means you.

Are you kidding me?

No. I'm too nervous to kid.

I mean, are you **KIDDING** me?

No?

Did you really spend three years talking to me about *another girl,* just to do... THIS on our last night?!

I guess so. Do you want me to stop?

It's just...

What if I don't like you that way? We're *friends,* you know?

Then we can both pretend this never happened?

Okay. Well... What if I *do* like you that way?

I don't know. I've never been in that situation before.

What if I liked you that way a long time ago, then got tired of waiting for you to take the hint?

I'm sorry, Deja. You know how dumb I am.

SNF SNF

SNORT!

What do we do now? I didn't rehearse this.

I think...

We go to Walgreens and buy half-priced candy.

Okay.

And...

STEP

And then we just see.

Deja, you taste like pumpkin.

Oh, man, now I'm never getting rid of you.

Try this.

CHOMP

Wow.

Right?

So, I was just talking to Marta who runs the Cookie Burrow? And she said we could take all of tonight's leftover pumpkin chip cookies...

Also, she told me she's got an in at the department store downtown—she might be able to get us temp jobs next month as Santa's elves.

Santa's elves?! I *love* Santa's elves!

Me, too!

Would we get those shoes? With the little bells?

And all the hot chocolate we can drink! She said a lot of college students work there over break.

RAINBOW ROWELL AND FAITH ERIN HICKS IN CONVERSATION

Rainbow: Faith! I'm trying to remember when we first met. I think it was on Twitter, after I read your book with Prudence Shen, *Nothing Could Possibly Go Wrong*. We bonded over our love for *Star Trek: The Next Generation*.

Faith: Yes, I remember that! It was pretty soon after San Diego Comic-Con, way back in 2013. I'd been a guest of the show (which was a magical experience) and I'd read your book *Eleanor & Park* on the flight from Halifax, Nova Scotia, to San Diego. I remember literally weeping over this book as I read it, which was actually the second time you'd made me cry. I'd read *Fangirl* earlier in the year and cried over that book, as well. I remember geeking out over your books on Twitter, and someone tweeted my fangirling at you and then eventually we started talking about Star Trek, the great icebreaker. I also remember getting up my courage to send you my graphic novel *Friends with Boys*, which I'd both written and drawn, and you were very kind about it. I really appreciated that.

So that's my memory of how we first met, but I'm trying to remember how you first got the idea to do a graphic novel. I think our publisher, First Second, saw that you were a comics fan and approached you. Is that correct?

Rainbow: ♥ ♥ ♥

You know, I think I connected with First Second on Twitter, too! Yeah, because I was a comics fan. Our editor, Calista Brill, was the person who suggested that you and I work together, and that immediately seemed like a good fit. I could see a lot of resonance between the types of stories that we both like to tell. All your books are very character driven and expressive, and you're especially good at capturing moments, I think. I felt like I could write a story that would feel like both of us.

Though I did initially pitch a totally different story!

Faith: The magic of the internet, haha. Just on a side note: I remember the story you originally pitched, and it was fascinating, but I also remember it had a lot of animals in it. I remember thinking, *Oh no, now I have to learn how to draw all these different animals!*

Pumpkinheads has a few animals (one in particular who plays a prominent role), but not nearly as many as your original story. So I was a bit relieved you changed your mind about what story you wanted to write, as I'm not great at drawing animals!

Rainbow: Ha, that's right. I'd forgotten about the animals! I had a few other story ideas that I played with for a while, too . . . To be honest, I was really sick at the time, and the other scripts I worked on reflected that; they were very heavy and blue, and I felt very heavy when I was working on them. I kept stalling out. Eventually, I decided that I needed to put my brain in a light and joyful place.

I had been hoarding this pumpkin patch setting for a few years. Like, I knew I wanted to do *something* with kids who work at a pumpkin patch. I broke the emergency glass on that idea, and the *Pumpkinheads* script came together so much more fluidly.

Faith: You sent me the script and I read it, and there was a part at the end where I totally teared up. And then drawing that scene was super emotional for me, as well! I don't normally think of myself as the kind of person who gets emotional over comic scripts, so having this reaction, I knew *Pumpkinheads* was special. I immediately sat down and did some rough sketches of Deja and Josiah. I was so eager to get them out of my head and on paper. It's funny looking back at those sketches now because the characters ended up looking so different in the book, but those awkward, early drawings are part of the development process. As characters they just leapt off the page at me. I immediately fell in love with both of them.

Rainbow: I was so relieved that they clicked with you right away. We'd agreed to work together before we had anything locked down—what if this script hadn't connected with you at all? *What if you hated pumpkins, Faith?*

Now that I've worked with a few other comic artists, I've noticed how I write differently depending on the artist, and depending on how well I know the artist. I was glad that I was familiar with your work, because it meant I could write with a lot of trust and confidence. I knew you'd bring so much chemistry to Deja and Josiah's relationship. And I knew that you'd just *nail* the pacing. (Which you did!)

Faith: Thank you! I was delighted with how you chose to write the script because you basically gave me a screenplay with dialogue, action, and emotional beats—but I got to do my own paneling and pacing for the comic. It's personally what I prefer, as I have Strong Opinions on paneling in comics, and how best to draw emotion out of the story. So that was something I really appreciated about collaborating with you on this story. You trusted me to do my thing.

Rainbow: But I did beg you to come to Omaha to visit my favorite pumpkin patch.

Faith: That was a really important trip for me. I don't think I'd have been able to draw the Patch as well as I did without that visit. I got to see the pumpkin patch as a real, lived-in place, full of people and delicious food.

Rainbow: It was very important for you to try Frito pie!

Faith: The Frito pie was very confusing for me at first! I have family in the States, but they're in the south, so I'm not familiar with Nebraska traditions. I was expecting this pie with, like, chips on top of it? And Frito pie is definitely not that. It's cheese and chips and other stuff in this little bag and you eat it with a fork. I remember asking, "When does it turn into pie?" Very confusing for the Canadian!

Rainbow: I think that trip really put us on the same page. We got to walk in Josiah and Deja's footsteps. Also, the script is set in an idealized, fictional pumpkin patch—like the Disneyland of pumpkin patches. So it helped to be in a similar environment and deciding, "Like this!" or "Not like this!" That's also where we had our first conversation about how important color would be in the book.

Thank you for making the trip. I owe you a trip to Canada. ♥

EARLY *PUMPKINHEADS* SKETCHES

Faith: These are the very first sketches of Deja and Josiah. They look so different here! We decided that they looked much too young in these early sketches, so I went back to the drawing board.

Rainbow: Look at these cuties! My script described Josiah as looking like Paul McCartney, and you can really see Faith trying that here. (I always think of Paul McCartney as having such a kind, gentle face!) Deja was described as "super-cute, like a chubby Gabrielle Union."

Rainbow: The main thing we talked about at this stage was making Josie and Deja look a little older. And I really wanted them to be close to the same height. I wanted to push back on the idea that a girl needs to be small and petite to be completely adorable.

Faith: I think of the character design process as a journey you go on with the characters: In the beginning you're trying to get to know them, who they are, and how best to draw them so their personalities comes through visually. And by time you've drawn the last page in their graphic novel, these characters are your best friends. You know them intimately as people, and that affects how you draw them.

ACKNOWLEDGMENTS

Faith and I would like to thank...

Everyone who helped us bring this book to life (and made the process an unusually joyful one!):

The biggest, shiniest thank-you to my best friend, Danielle Henderson, for inspiring all of Deja's most luminous moments.

And thank you to Leigh Bardugo and Samantha Irby for reading and discussing and actually coming to visit me in Omaha. (I owe you both infinite favors and pumpkin chocolate chip cookies.)

Thank you to Christopher Schelling, who still has *not* come to Omaha, but provided as much encouragement and good advice as he could from Connecticut.

Thank you *like whoa* to Faith's remarkable agent, Bernadette Baker-Baughman; to our editor, Calista Brill, and the crackerjack team at First Second Books; to Sarah Stern, whose colors made this the most *beautiful* pumpkin patch in the world; and especially to the scrupulous Rachel Stark, who came along just when we needed her.

The pumpkin patch in this book is fictional, but Omaha really does have the best pumpkin patches in the world (Faith can attest to this!), and I sincerely hope you get to visit one someday.

Rainbow

First Second

Don't miss your next favorite book from First Second!
For the latest updates go to firstsecondnewsletter.com and sign up for our enewsletter.

Published by First Second
First Second is an imprint of Roaring Brook Press,
a division of Holtzbrinck Publishing Holdings Limited Partnership
120 Broadway, New York, NY 10271
All rights reserved

Library of Congress Control Number: 2018944911

Paperback ISBN: 978-1-62672-162-3
Hardcover ISBN: 978-1-250-31285-3

Our books may be purchased in bulk for promotional, educational, or business use.
Please contact your local bookseller or the Macmillan Corporate and
Premium Sales Department at (800) 221-7945 ext. 5442 or by
email at MacmillanSpecialMarkets@macmillan.com.

First edition, 2019

Edited by Calista Brill and Rachel Stark
Book design by Molly Johanson
Interior color by Sarah Stern
Color assistance by K Uvick and Sammy Savos
Cover color by Shelli Paroline and Braden Lamb

Penciled digitally in Manga Studio on a Wacom Cintiq.
Inked traditionally with a Raphaël Kolinsky watercolor brush.
Colored digitally in Photoshop.

Printed in China
Paperback: 10 9 8 7 6 5 4 3 2 1
Hardcover: 10 9 8 7 6 5 4 3 2 1